# CREEPY CREATURES

# BAT ATTACK

Collect all the
# CREEPY CREATURES

# CREEPY CREATURES

# BAT ATTACK
## ED GRAVES

SCHOLASTIC

*With special thanks to Tracey Turner*

First published in the UK in 2011 by Scholastic Children's Books
An imprint of Scholastic Ltd
Euston House, 24 Eversholt Street
London, NW1 1DB, UK
Registered office: Westfield Road, Southam, Warwickshire, CV47 0RA
SCHOLASTIC and associated logos are trademarks and/or registered
trademarks of Scholastic Inc.
Series created by Working Partners Ltd

Text copyright © Working Partners, 2011
The right of Ed Graves to be identified as the author of this work
has been asserted by him.

ISBN 978 1407 11713 3

Printed in the UK by CPI Bookmarque, Croydon, Surrey.
Papers used by Scholastic Children's Books are made
from wood grown in sustainable forests.

1 3 5 7 9 10 8 6 4 2

www.scholastic.co.uk/zone

*For Toby Battersby and Wilma Zapper*

## This Book Belongs To

_The Gnome of Gnome Gardens_

Beware!
Never open my Book, unless you
want the Curse of Gnome upon you.
Or is it too late?
Then my creatures will terrify
and torment you.
You can't imagine how scared you will be.
Gnome Gardens belongs to me.
Only me. You shall see. . .

# CHAPTER ONE

## A Storm at Gnome Gardens

A fork of lightning raced across the afternoon sky, lighting up the turrets and gargoyles of Gnome Gardens. Jamie looked up at the enormous old house, with its ivy-covered walls and windows like scowling eyes. He found it hard to believe that Gnome Gardens was his home now. Then – *crash!* – a great roll of thunder boomed in his ears. Rain burst from the swollen clouds, drenching him, his brother Harry and their friend Milly.

"Quick!" Milly shouted, her hair plastered to her face by the rain. "Get inside!" She ran for the path.

Jamie threw down his rake. The three of them had been tidying the neglected vegetable patch in Jamie and Harry's vast, overgrown garden. Now rain water turned the earth to thick mud, washing away the seeds they'd planted. A sudden gust of wind sent the cracked windows of the greenhouse rattling in their frames.

Jamie squelched through the soil to join Milly. His muddy trainers slipped on the wet moss on the paving stones.

"Come on, Harry!" he called to his brother.

Harry was still standing in the sticky mud, staring up at the sky and hugging his arms to his chest. Jamie shivered as the wind howled around him, bending the trees and tearing the leaves from their branches. The leaves swooped and fluttered through the air, like a flock of tiny creatures in the gloomy sky.

"Bats!" Harry shouted, as the leaves swirled. "They've come to get us already!" He ran towards Jamie and Milly, mud splattering his jeans.

"Harry, they're just leaves!" Jamie called, shouting to be heard above the wind.

But Jamie knew why his brother was scared of seeing bats. In the study at the centre of

Gnome Gardens, the boys had found *The Book of Gnome*, which was written by Jamie and Harry's granddad. The book told the story of the evil Gnome who thought he owned their house. The Gnome had already sent two of his creepy creatures to drive them out – a monstrous snake and a giant spider. The book's ancient pages had shown them that the next creature they would meet was an evil-looking, yellow-eyed bat, its leathery wings outstretched, its ugly snout curled into a snarl that revealed sharp fangs. Underneath the picture was a single line: *Fear the bats up above*. Jamie shivered. No wonder Harry was so jumpy.

"Hurry up," Jamie said. He led his brother and Milly as they slithered up the path.

All three of them cried out as a fork of

lightning shot down in front of them. The old, dead tree in the middle of the garden sizzled. They froze, staring at the smoking branches, a great roar of thunder echoing in their ears.

There was a loud crack.

"Look out!" shouted Jamie, grabbing Milly and Harry and pulling them backwards. A huge branch fell from the tree and crashed to the ground, missing them by centimetres.

Milly's face was white with shock. "Thanks. That was a close one." She grabbed Harry's hand and with the other pushed Jamie along. "Let's go. We have to get inside before the lightning strikes again."

"This is just the sort of time the Gnome would choose to come for us," Harry said, the rain running down his face and dripping off the end of his nose. "The middle of a storm."

Jamie saw his brother reach behind him for the backpack he always carried. It contained his "survival kit" – odds and ends that Harry thought might be useful. Jamie was sure that, no matter what Harry had put in his backpack this time, none of it would be much use if the Gnome attacked now. The three of them had vowed to defeat him, but Jamie didn't want to have to try in the middle of a raging storm.

They reached the end of the path. Gnome Gardens was on top of the hill, but Milly's cottage was through a gate on the other side of the garden.

"I'll see you tomorrow," Milly shouted over

the storm. "Don't stand under any trees – you've more chance of being struck by lightning. And keep low to the ground!"

"Be careful, Milly!" shouted Harry.

But before she left the path, a chilling sound rose above the howling wind and lashing rain. The three of them stared, open-mouthed, at one another.

It was the unmistakable sound of the Gnome's evil laughter.

# CHAPTER TWO

## Shapes in the Shadows

"Wh-what's that?" Harry said, his voice quavering. He was staring into the bushes on the other side of the path.

Jamie peered into the undergrowth. Something – a low, dark shape – was stalking towards them. His heart pounded. Was the Gnome coming for them?

Milly took a step back. "We have to hide. Behind that wall!"

They ran through tall, wet grass to a crumbling brick wall only a few strides away. They scrambled behind it and crouched down. Jamie carefully peeped around the wall, at the bushes. There was definitely something there, a dark shadow among the leaves. A flash of red, two darting bright circles. . .

A fox! It emerged, sopping wet, its ears back against its head. It loped across the garden and away through a hedge.

Jamie let out a long breath.

"Phew!" Milly said, forcing a laugh. "I thought it might be a fox." Jamie knew she was pretending to be brave now, but he wasn't fooled. She smiled weakly at him.

*I won't say anything*, he thought, smiling back. There was no point making her feel embarrassed as well as scared.

"We heard the Gnome, though," Harry said. "He could still be here, hiding somewhere. Anywhere."

"Harry's right," Jamie said. "We have to be ready for him."

"He'll want his revenge for what you did to that spider," Harry said to him.

Jamie had snapped one of the legs off the Gnome's horrible spider as it tried to grab Harry.

"How do we know the Gnome won't come for one of us in the night?" Harry continued, hugging his backpack. "He could send his horrible bat – it could fly through the window. Maybe it's a vampire bat—"

"We could send a signal to each other," Milly said quickly.

"Torches!" Jamie said. "We can see each other's windows. At midnight, we'll flash our torch three times from our house – that means everything's OK. Then Milly can send three flashes back from hers, to say she's all right too."

"Right," Milly said, "see you at midnight. Or see your torch, anyway. Now let's get out of this storm."

Milly set off down the hill to Gardener's Cottage, while Jamie and Harry broke into a run up the hill towards Gnome Gardens, their feet slapping loudly against the wet flagstones. The rain pelted down, splashing into the old stone bird bath, hammering on the roof of the ruined well as they jogged past it. Jamie shivered. The well was where they'd met the Gnome's giant snake. They were going to have to be brave when they faced the Gnome and his creatures again.

"Race you over there!" Harry shouted, sprinting ahead towards a low, sagging fence, only just visible above the long grass.

Jamie caught up with him and hurdled it, his trainers skidding on the sodden grass on the other side. Harry jumped too, but his body jerked as something caught at his leg, and he landed on his hands and knees.

"Ow! Get off me!" he shouted.

Jamie ran over to his brother. A vicious-looking creeper covered in sharp spines was coiled round Harry's ankle. Its stem snaked through the long grass to an overgrown flower bed. There Jamie could see its roots, sticking up through the soil like a gnarled hand.

*It looks like it's lying in wait for someone to grab*, he thought. He yanked the creeper away from Harry's leg, wincing as the thorns dug into his fingers.

"Just stay calm," Jamie told Harry, despite the rain soaking through his clothes. "I'll have this off you in a minute."

Lightning crackled above them, illuminating the sky in another bright flash. Jamie and Harry looked up.

A huge, dark shape was silhouetted against the swollen clouds, its wings outstretched.

"It's the Gnome's bat!" yelled Harry over the boom of thunder.

The thing swooped across the sky and

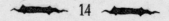

into the clouds, out of sight, letting out an eerie shriek. Jamie shuddered. *So that's what we'll have to fight*, he thought grimly.

He looked down the hill towards Milly's house. Milly was standing in her garden, the rain drenching her, staring up into the sky. *She must have seen it too*, Jamie thought. She turned and looked towards them, waved, then ran into her house.

Jamie looked up again: nothing, just the heavy clouds and leaves tossed about by the wind.

"Jamie, let's get home before that thing comes back!" Harry cried, pulling Jamie's arm. They turned towards Gnome Gardens and sprinted up the path.

Jamie reached for the big brass door handle but, before he could touch it, the door flew open, sucking a flurry of leaves into the house. Jamie fell inside, pulled Harry in after him and slammed the door behind them, shutting out the noise of the howling wind. They both leaned against it, panting for breath, their sodden clothes dripping on the floor.

Jamie ran a hand through his soaking hair. Somewhere, the radio was playing Mum's favourite song above the sound of the washing machine. Jamie breathed in a delicious smell: baking bread.

"Jamie? Harry? You haven't been out in this storm, have you?" Mum called to them from the kitchen.

"Er. . . That bread smells good – can we give you a hand?" Jamie called back.

"What have you two been up to?" Mum

called again. Jamie and Harry looked at each other guiltily.

"Dodging lightning," Harry whispered.

"Shhh!" Jamie said, a finger to his lips. "Don't say anything to Mum."

"How are we going to explain our wet clothes?" Harry hissed back. Jamie looked down at his rain-soaked jeans.

"Come on. Let's get changed first. Then we'll go and help Mum." He ran up the stairs, with Jamie following, and the two of them disappeared into their rooms.

The storm still hadn't stopped. Jamie looked up from his comic as the rain drove against his bedroom window. He peered out through the ivy but he could barely see anything in the lashing rain and gathering dusk. Wind shook the glass and whistled through the gaps in the window frame, sending a cold, damp draught into the room. Jamie could hear the rain gurgling along the gutters and down the drainpipes.

*It's nearly night-time*, Jamie thought. *I hope Milly's OK.*

Harry came into the bedroom, the tip of his tongue poking out of the corner of his mouth. He was balancing a plate of the bread that Mum had been baking. The thick slices were smeared with golden butter.

"Here," he said. "Mum's just cut it."

Dad poked his head around the door and grabbed the top slice. "Thanks!" he said.

"Oi!" said Harry, grinning.

Dad was holding up a model steam train and a length of track. "Look. I found this in a cupboard upstairs. There's a whole train set, loads of it, with stations and proper points and signals. Must have been your granddad's."

"Wow," Harry said. "I've always wanted one of those. Does it work?"

"I'll set it up and find out. It should do – but it's old; it might need a bit of fiddling with."

"Can we help?" Harry asked.

"You can," said Dad, "but it might take a while. Perhaps you could do some exploring – there's a picture gallery where I found this. I'll let you know when the train set's ready."

"Where's the gallery?" Jamie asked.

"In the attic, right at the top of the house," Dad said. "It's full of old portraits – and some of the people in them look pretty creepy. You'll love it." He smiled.

Jamie and Harry exchanged a glance. *Dad would be surprised at the creepy things we've already seen in this house*, Jamie thought.

"OK, we'll go and explore," he said. "Give us a shout if you need a hand."

As Dad left, Jamie noticed something out of the corner of his eye: something fluttering. He spun round. A piece of paper drifted down from the ceiling and landed on his pillow.

"Did you see that?" Harry asked. "What is it?"

Jamie frowned. He picked up the yellowed piece of paper from his pillow and turned it over.

There was a message, in big, black letters. It was one he'd seen before:

**FEAR THE BATS UP ABOVE.**

# CHAPTER THREE

# The Grim Gallery

The main staircase of Gnome Gardens swept from the hallway to the first floor, where Jamie and Harry's bedroom was, then narrowed as it curved upwards. As the boys climbed to the third floor, the staircase was only just wide enough for the two of them to go side by side. It was covered in dust from long years of disuse and the steps creaked loudly. Jamie held the plate of bread and butter, which they had brought with them in case they got hungry.

"Lots of spiders up here," said Harry, touching an ancient cobweb hanging from the banisters. Jamie nodded. Ordinary spiders didn't bother them any more, no matter how big they were – not after their encounter with the Gnome's giant spider.

The gallery was one of the rooms in the old house that Jamie and Harry had never even seen. The house was so big that when they'd first moved in, Mum and Dad had shut lots of rooms up until they could make sure they were safe. Some of the rooms had rotten windows, just waiting to fall out completely, or buckets filling up with water from leaks in the roof. During their first days in the house, Jamie and Harry had found a secret passage leading to their granddad's old study. Jamie thought there might be others, waiting to be discovered.

"Look, Jamie." Harry held out his hand, black with dust where he'd gripped the banister. Then he glanced at the stairs. "Lizards!" he said.

Reptiles slithered down the edges of the stairs, carved into the wood. The whole house was full of strange carvings. Jamie ran his finger along a lizard's scaly tail. It looked almost real, as if it might start thrashing from side to side at any moment. "And ants, beetles and worms," he said, pointing out the wooden creatures swarming up the skirting boards. *No bats, though*, thought Jamie. *At least, not yet.*

"Bats live at the tops of buildings, don't they?" said Harry. "Don't they live in belfries? I bet there's a belfry in this house. Whatever that is," he added.

"No, there isn't," said Jamie. "A belfry's for church bells." Then he noticed something out of the corner of his eye and spun around. A small pair of eyes stared down at him from the shadowy ceiling. He looked more closely . . . then felt a huge shove in his back.

"Quick! Run!" Harry was pushing him up the stairs. "It's a bat!"

Jamie sprinted up the twisting staircase to a small landing, then tripped over the final step, struggling not to drop his plate of bread and butter. Harry collapsed on top of him. Jamie peered round the banister to see if the bat was following them, his heart thumping.

There was a bat on the ceiling, its jaws open and its clawed wings stretched wide – but it was only a carving. Jamie sighed with relief. They didn't have to face the Gnome just yet.

Harry had his arms over his head. "Has it gone?" he asked.

"It's all right. It's just a carving." Jamie got to his feet and pulled his brother up.

"Well, it looked real," Harry said sheepishly. "Imagine one of them coming for us, with its nasty wings and teeth . . . I'm going back down." He turned to go downstairs.

"Don't be silly, Harry," Jamie said. "It's made of wood."

Harry hung back, looking unsure.

"Don't you want to see the gallery?" Jamie persisted, holding his brother's arm. Harry slowly put his foot on the next step.

They climbed the last short flight of stairs. On the small landing, a heavy wooden door was propped open by a brass doorstop in the shape of a fat toad. The open door revealed bare floorboards, cracked and dusty.

"What's that?" Harry said. There was a strange howling noise echoing from inside the room. And it sounded as though something was tapping at one of the windows.

Jamie gulped and peered into the gallery. "It's the storm," he said. "The wind's howling down the chimney, that's all. And there's ivy at the window." He took a few cautious steps into the room. "Come on."

The floorboards creaked as Jamie walked across the gallery. It was a long, narrow room, with huge windows as tall as Jamie on one side, and portraits in ornate gold frames on the other. There was a tattered old standard lamp, and next to it a seat that ran along the bottom of one of the windows. Jamie put the plate of bread down on a faded cushion and looked at the portraits. His gaze was met by the forbidding stares of elderly gentlemen in old-fashioned black coats, children with little dogs, and old ladies in long, black dresses. They all peered down at Jamie with cold, sad eyes. The paintings were yellowed with age, their frames hung with cobwebs. One picture, of a severe-looking man in a top hat, had long scratches on it like claw marks.

"Look at this one, it's got a skull in it,"

Harry said, stopping in front of a portrait of a thin man with a hooked nose. On a table in front of him was a grey human skull and two dead partridges. "No wonder he looks so miserable."

Rain hammered against the windows and the ivy tapped, as if desperate to come inside. Jamie looked out: soon it would be dark.

"Do you think Milly will be all right?" Harry asked.

"She'll be OK. She's tough," Jamie said.

He shivered as he paused in front of the largest painting in the room. Instead of a person, this portrait was of a huge bat, hanging upside down from a branch. Its leathery wings were spread wide, its hook-like claws glinting. Its yellow eyes seemed to stare out at Jamie.

"Hey, Harry," he said, trying to keep his voice steady. "Does this remind you of anything?"

"The bat picture in *The Book of Gnome*," said Harry. Jamie could hear him gulp. "And look at this." Harry was pointing at the window, where three small bats had been carved into the woodwork, hanging upside down from the sill. He took a step back. "They're everywhere!"

Jamie looked at the panelled walls. Bats swooped and soared across them, carefully sculpted into the wood. The fireplace was covered in bat carvings too – some of them hung by their feet from the mantlepiece. He felt goosebumps prickle on his arms.

Harry clutched Jamie's shoulder. "Remember the snake carvings coming to life?" he said, his face pale. "Maybe the bats will come alive too." He looked at the fireplace. "The Gnome could be hiding in the chimney, like he did in the nursery," he said.

Jamie ducked and peered up into the dark chimney flue. Nothing. He put his hand inside it, dislodging clumps of grime, and showed Harry his blackened hand. "Just a load of old soot." He made a grab for Harry with his sooty hand.

"Aargh! Get off!" Harry twisted away from Jamie and ran to the other end of the gallery, his footsteps echoing around the empty room. Jamie raced after him, laughing. They made three circuits of the room before Harry collapsed on the window seat. He picked up a slice of bread from the plate Jamie had put there and shoved it into his mouth. The butter melted against his tongue and the bread was still warm from the oven. Jamie sat down beside him, wiping his hands on his jeans.

The fading daylight sparkled against something above the fireplace. It was another picture, with an elaborate frame studded with coloured jewels that glimmered yellow, red and green. *They're the Gnome's colours*, Jamie thought, swallowing. *He likes shiny things like those jewels. Could they be something to do with him?*

The painting showed a landscape of trees, fields and distant houses. But there was something odd about it.

"Jamie. The picture. . ." Harry was staring at it too. "It's moving!" He dropped the piece of bread he'd been eating.

In the painting, thunder clouds swirled across the scene. The tops of the trees were swaying and a tractor toiled up a hill. *Could this be more of the Gnome's magic?* Jamie wondered. He walked towards the picture to look more closely, then saw . . . himself. "It's a mirror!" he said, feeling silly. He was just seeing a reflection of the fields outside.

Harry laughed. He looked from the mirror to the view from the window of swirling storm clouds, driving rain and shivering trees. "Hey!" he cried suddenly. "This is the perfect place to signal to Milly! There's her house. We can see it much better from here than we can from our room."

Jamie breathed on the glass, then rubbed with his sleeve to wipe away the dirt. He peered through the smeared glass. There was Milly's cheerful-looking cottage, with its red roof and white shutters, a climbing rose framing the front door. *It couldn't be more different from Gnome Gardens*, he thought.

"Boys!" Dad's voice echoed up the stairs. "Train set's ready!"

"Come on," Jamie said, relieved to be leaving the gallery. He leaped down from the window seat, snatching up the last slice of bread and butter.

"Race you down!" Harry was already bolting for the door.

Jamie ran after him. Just as he reached the door, a cold prickle of fear ran down his spine. Was something watching him? He looked back into the room. In the portrait, the bat's yellow eyes seemed to flicker. *Must be my imagination*, he thought. He held the bat's gaze for a second: he knew they'd have to face the Gnome's creature soon. Would they be ready?

# CHAPTER FOUR

# Midnight in the Gallery

Jamie sat on the edge of his bed, gazing out of his bedroom window. The night was dark, with just the barest glimmer of the moon behind thick clouds. The storm had passed, but rain still gurgled along the ancient drainpipes and wet leaves clung to the windowpanes.

"Hurry up," Jamie said. "We've got to get to the gallery by midnight, or Milly will wonder what's happened to us."

Harry stuffed a torch into his backpack, zipped it up and pulled it on over his pyjamas. He looked as though he were about to climb a mountain. "Ready!"

Jamie smiled. "Come on, then."

On the landing they paused, listening for Dad's telltale snoring, which would let them know the coast was clear. Sure enough, long, noisy snores rumbled through their parents' bedroom door. They crept past it and along the corridor, the dusty floorboards chilly on Jamie's bare feet. They tried not to make a sound but it seemed that every step they took set off a loud creak.

"Mmmf!" Harry gave a muffled cry.

Jamie swivelled round to see his brother balancing on one leg, rubbing his other foot. Jamie could see a toy car on the floor that Harry must have trodden on. The snoring stopped. Jamie held his breath, sure that Mum and Dad would wake up. But their bedroom door stayed shut. The snoring started up again. Jamie let out a breath and rolled his eyes at Harry. Then he nodded at the staircase, a finger to his lips, and began to climb.

*Creak!*

"Stay on the side nearest the banisters," Jamie whispered in Harry's ear. "It doesn't make as much noise."

There was a long groaning sound from somewhere above them, like a door opening slowly on rusty hinges. Jamie stopped, clinging to the banisters, his heart thumping loudly in his chest.

"What was that?" whispered Harry. The whites of his eyes were bright in the darkness.

There were more creaks, a thump as if something had fallen on to the floorboards, a scuttling sound – and then silence.

"It's just the house settling," said Jamie. He relaxed his hold on the railing. "Dad's always complaining about the water pipes rattling."

Harry looked doubtful, but he followed Jamie up the next flight of stairs.

Jamie was ready for the carved bat's ugly snout and outstretched wings as it loomed at him in the darkness, but still his stomach lurched for a second. He and Harry hurried past it.

"We've made it!" whispered Jamie as they reached the top of the stairs. Then he froze. The door to the gallery was shut. In front of it, the toad doorstop was overturned. It rocked slightly from side to side, then lay still.

Jamie and Harry looked at each other uneasily.

"Did you shut the door this afternoon?" asked Harry.

Jamie shook his head.

"Then who did? And who moved the toad? Who—?"

"We're running out of time," Jamie interrupted him. "Milly will be waiting. Come on, we have to go inside."

He turned the large brass door handle, but it wouldn't budge. He put his shoulder to it and pushed. The door was stuck.

Both of them put their hands against the door and shoved. It didn't move, but Jamie felt something round under his fingers. He moved his hand – another carving. He stepped back to look at it.

"What's up?" Harry asked.

Carved into the thick wooden door was a familiar bearded face, wearing a cap. It was deeply wrinkled, with a bulbous nose and small, staring eyes. The lips were drawn back into a cruel sneer. Jamie felt a chill run down his back.

"The Gnome," Harry said. "It's a sure sign he's around."

Jamie swallowed hard. "The door was open before – I suppose that's why we didn't see it."

"What shall we do?" Harry's face was pale.

"Whatever's in there, we have to face it sometime. And we can't break our promise to Milly," Jamie said.

Harry picked at the rough, orange-tinged hinges. "I don't understand," he said. "How could they have got so rusty since this afternoon?"

*The Gnome must have done it*, thought Jamie. Aloud, he asked, "What's in your backpack? Anything that could help?"

Harry took off the backpack and rummaged inside it. He made a sheepish face as he brought out a package wrapped in greaseproof paper and handed it to Jamie.

"Not *more* bread and butter, Harry!" Jamie said as he opened it. "You've already eaten half a loaf!"

"It's not for me!" Harry exclaimed. "Couldn't we use the butter as grease?"

"You're a genius." Jamie grinned, scraping some of it on to his fingers. "We can use this to get the door open." He smeared the butter on the rusty hinges.

The two of them gave the door another big shove.

With a dull groan and a long creak, the door swung open. The boys fell forward into the room, looking around quickly for any sign of the Gnome.

The room had to be dark for Milly to see their torch signal, but they still needed a bit of light to see. Jamie flicked on the lamp. It cast a weak glow around the dusty room, lighting the faces in the portraits so that the eyes seemed to flicker. Jamie glanced at the bat painting. Its yellow eyes, fangs and claws looked even more real in the dim light.

A loud clang rang out. The church bell was chiming midnight.

"Quick!" Jamie said, rushing over to the window seat. "The torch – before Milly wonders what's happened to us. I can see a light in her window – she's waiting."

Harry delved into his backpack again.

Jamie looked out of the window into the darkness. He was deliberately not looking at the bat painting, but his spine tingled, and he had the same feeling of being watched that he'd had earlier. "Come on, Harry," he said. "What have you *got* in there?"

Just as the sound of the bell began to fade away, Harry brought out the torch and flicked it on – straight into Jamie's face.

"Shine it out of the window!" hissed Jamie, shielding his eyes and pushing the torch away. "Three flashes, remember?"

Harry's hands were trembling, but he managed to point the torch the right way. He turned it off, on, off, on, off, on. . . "One, two, three!" Harry said. "That's it!"

Jamie held his breath.

The light in Milly's window flashed.

"There!" Harry said, turning to Jamie with a grin. "Milly's OK!"

The light flashed again.

"That's two," said Jamie.

But then there was nothing. The cottage remained dark.

Jamie and Harry stared at each other.

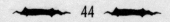

"Jamie? Why hasn't she sent the third signal?" said Harry in a small voice. "What's the Gnome done to her?"

# CHAPTER FIVE

# The Flight of the Bats

Jamie struggled to heave up the old sash window. It stuck in the frame as he jiggled it from side to side.

"Quick! Come on!" cried Harry.

Jamie gave an extra-strong shove and the frame flew up so quickly that he almost fell out into the rainy night. Harry caught hold of his pyjamas and dragged him back inside. The two of them stared out into the darkness.

"Milly!" he shouted across the garden.

There was no reply. He looked around desperately. A startled owl swooped out of one of the tall trees.

"Milly!" he called again, Harry's voice joining his. A fox ran across the overgrown lawn, low to the ground. It stared up at them, its ears pricked.

Then Jamie heard a scratching, scrabbling sound above them. He looked up.

Something was moving in the eaves of Gnome Gardens, directly above the gallery window. A blur of leathery wings, sharp teeth and flashing claws.

"Bats!" shouted Harry.

Three of the creatures swooped down. They flew straight towards the open window, their beady eyes fixed on Jamie, then wheeled away. A moment later, more bats joined them, then more still, billowing out from the eaves like dark clouds. They swooped in a long, fluttering stream across the garden, away from the house.

"Hundreds of them!" Harry said, staring through the window. "Where are they going? The Gnome will send them back here and make them *do* something to us! Maybe they'll suck our blood—"

"Shhh! We need to listen out for Milly!" hissed Jamie. His heart was pounding. What had happened to their friend?

They tried calling again but Milly didn't answer. Jamie leaned out dangerously far over the window frame. He could only hear the soft swish of the trees and the splash of the falling rain.

"Jamie, look!" Harry cried, pointing.

A dark shape was silhouetted against the moon. Jamie blinked and struggled to make out what it was. As the shape moved towards them, he realized it was the bats. They were coming back — and they held something as they flew. What were they carrying? It looked like . . . like a girl! *No, it can't be*, thought Jamie.

"Help!" Milly's cry rang across the garden.

Jamie felt his heart lurch. The bats were gripping Milly with their claws. Some held on to her pyjamas, some to her hair. They swooped upwards, higher and higher, over the treetops. Milly cried out as she brushed the top of the oak tree. Jamie imagined her looking down to the garden far below, knowing the bats might drop her at any moment. They circled the garden, passing so close to Jamie and Harry that they could see Milly's terrified face. Tears streaked her cheeks and Jamie could see her hairline pulling where the bats' claws were tangled in her plaits.

"Milly! We'll help you!" shouted Jamie.

"How?" Harry yelped, staring at the bats as they swooped around the garden.

"Put me down!" Milly shouted. "I said, put me down!"

The bats turned again. This time they were heading straight for the open window. They suddenly flew forward, aiming straight for them like a huge dark arrow puncturing the sky. Jamie could see the yellow eyes of the ones at the front.

"Out of the way, Harry!" Jamie cried, leaping aside as the bats flew into the gallery. Jamie crouched down as they flapped, shrieking, above his head, a black wave of them blocking the moonlight as they hurtled into the room. He could see the glint of their teeth, their lips pulled back from their jaws. Tiny claws at the end of their leathery wings sliced the air. Their horrible screeching rang in his ears. Harry crouched beside him and threw his hands over his head, squeezing his eyes tight shut. Jamie reached out for Millie as she flew over him but the bats held her too tightly and whisked her away. Her feet kicked against empty air.

"Get off me! Put me down!" shouted Milly, as the bats circled the room.

Harry's eyes snapped open. He leaped to his feet and jumped, trying to grab her. "Don't worry, Milly! We'll get them off you!" he called. But his hands closed on nothing as she was carried high above him.

Jamie stood on the window seat and clutched at Milly as she passed. For a moment he grasped her ankles, but the bats snatched her away again, keeping her just out of reach.

"Jamie! Harry!" Milly cried, twisting and turning in the bats' grip.

The bats fluttered up to the ceiling, shrieking delightedly as if they were playing a game; then there was a moment's silence and they all released their grip, letting her go.

With a cry, Milly dropped on to the floor. She landed with a thud and lay there, her arms stretched out awkwardly in front of her. Jamie and Harry leaped down beside her and each took an arm. Her body was heavy and lifeless, but they pulled her upright.

Milly's tear-stained, pale face was scratched.

"Milly! Are you all right?" said Jamie.

She nodded and wiped her face with her pyjama sleeve. The colour was returning to her cheeks. "They flew through my bedroom window and grabbed me. I couldn't fight them off." She scowled at the bats. A cloud of them had settled on the ceiling, while some hung upside down from the picture rail. Others clung to the mantlepiece and the sides of the mirror, encased in leathery wings.

*Smash!* The sash window slammed back down on to the sill, the glass splintering in the frame and crashing to the floor. A cold gust of wind blew into the room. Jamie shivered, his arm still around Milly. He could feel her shaking.

The noise seemed to startle the bats, which took flight again. They swooped around the room, gathering together and swirling in front of the huge painting of the bat. Jamie could see the hooked claws on their wings and sharp little teeth when they opened their mouths to screech.

Above the sound of the shrieking bats echoed familiar, wicked laughter. It seemed to mock them.

"It's him!" said Harry, his voice trembling.

All three of them whirled around, expecting to see the Gnome step out of the shadows. But he was nowhere to be seen. Jamie shone the torch into the corners of the room where the lamplight barely reached, the torch beam flickering as his hand shook. But it only lit dusty, cobwebby corners . . . and more bats. He pointed the torch at the bat portrait. Its yellow eyes shone in the ray of light.

Then the eyes in the portrait blinked. Jamie stared, the blood chilling in his veins. One of the eyes winked at him.

Jamie dropped the torch.

"You don't listen, do you?" said a cruel, sneering voice from behind the painting. "I told you – Gnome Gardens is mine."

"It's the Gnome," said Milly shakily. Jamie could feel Harry clutching his arm.

"But you're still here, aren't you?" the Gnome continued, sounding furious now. "You're still in my house. But you're about to regret it, you little wretches." He spat out the words.

Suddenly a flash of lightning lit up the room. A great crack of thunder boomed and rain came hammering through the broken window. With a fizz and a pop, the lamp went out. They were plunged into inky darkness.

# CHAPTER SIX

## The Bats Attack

Without the dim lamplight Jamie could hardly see. He heard Milly gasp, and Harry whimpered beside him, still clutching his arm. All around them, Jamie heard shrill squeaks and the swish of leathery wings. Something passed close by in front of his face and he felt a cold breeze. The bats were swooping around the room.

"Get off!" Jamie shouted, throwing up his arms as a bat brushed against his scalp.

He heard the Gnome laugh from his hiding place behind the portrait.

One of the bats clipped Jamie's face with its wing – then another, and another, their tiny claws scratching his head.

"They're all over me!" shouted Harry.

Jamie reached for his brother and Milly in the darkness. "Stay close together," he said.

They huddled on the ground, their arms over their heads to shield themselves. Jamie could feel the bats' disgusting furry bodies as they brushed against his arms and back, the nip of little fangs, the touch of the stretched skin of their wings. Several of them landed on Jamie's shoulders, biting through his clothes. Their attackers let out hisses and squeals of delight.

"Get off!" Milly shouted, swiping at the creatures.

Every time Jamie flapped his arms to wave the bats away, more of them flew at his face, scratching with their claws and biting. It was impossible. "Head for the door!" he cried. "We have to get out!"

Harry let out a yelp. In the dim moonlight, Jamie saw his brother rise above him. Harry seemed to be getting taller, his frightened face surrounded by bats.

"They've got me!" he screamed. "Jamie!"

Jamie grabbed at Harry's pyjamas but, with a rush of air, Harry was whipped away from him. The bats flew with Harry to the ceiling, holding on to his clothes with their claws.

Milly leaped as high as she could but Harry was out of her reach. The bats whirled him around the room above their heads, shrieking horribly.

"They're biting me!" Harry cried.

The bats flew up and up, high above Jamie's head. For the first time Jamie noticed the panelled wooden ceiling of the room – that was engraved with bats, too!

"Drop!" the Gnome snarled from behind the portrait.

The bats all let go. Harry gave a piercing scream as he fell to the floor.

"Catch!" ordered the Gnome.

As one, the bats darted down and grabbed Harry just before he hit the floor, and circled the room again. They'd do whatever the Gnome told them. He gave a wicked laugh.

"Harry!" Jamie ran around the room, reaching out for his brother. *Maybe they really will drop him next time*, he thought grimly. Milly fended off a cloud of bats as she jumped to catch hold of Harry's leg. But the creatures were too quick for her and whisked him away.

"Help! Jamie!" Harry was screaming now.

Desperately, Jamie leaped into the air and made another lunge at his brother. His fingers closed around one of the straps on Harry's backpack. "I've got you, Harry!"

Milly grabbed the other strap. "Call off your bats, Gnome!" she yelled.

"Not until you leave my house," the Gnome snarled.

Jamie felt his jaw set with determination.

"Pull!" he cried. He and Milly yanked at Harry's backpack, wrenching him from the bats' grasp.

Harry landed in a heap on the floor by the fireplace, sobbing. Jamie and Milly both put an arm around him.

"We've got you," Milly said, wiping his eyes with her sleeve. "Don't worry."

The bats flapped away, gathering close to the ceiling, screeching shrilly. *Preparing for another attack*, thought Jamie, gingerly touching the scratches on his face. He could see the three of them reflected in the mirror above the fireplace, sitting huddled together on the floorboards, shaking, tear-stained and covered in scratches. The jewels on the mirror's frame shone in the moonlight. He remembered the note that had fluttered to the floor in their bedroom. What had it said? *Fear the bats up above.* They were frightened now, no doubt about that!

Something was scuffling behind the bat painting. The canvas started to bulge and buckle, so that the bat looked as though it was moving its wings. There was a scratching sound; then the painting tore as the Gnome's gnarled fist punched its way through. Filthy yellow fingernails ripped at the tear in the canvas. Jamie could hear the Gnome grunting with effort.

"The Gnome's coming to get us," whimpered Harry. "What are we going to do?"

Jamie looked around the room. His gaze came to rest on the jewels in the frame of the mirror. Shiny, glistening jewels. . . "I've got an idea!" he cried. "Quick – where's the torch?"

"There!" Harry spotted where it had rolled on the floor by the skirting board. He grabbed it and handed it to Jamie, his hand trembling.

"Remember the scissors we found in the chimney shaft?" Jamie said. "We know the Gnome loves sparkly things. He won't be able to resist the jewels in the mirror – especially when I shine the torch at them."

"Good idea! Come on," Milly said, scrambling back. "We don't want to be too near the Gnome. Let's go to the other end of the room, away from the mirror."

They ran to the other end of the gallery. Jamie switched on the torch and a golden-yellow shaft of light punctured the air. He held the torch in front of his chest, aiming the beam straight at the ornate mirror. He blinked as the light bounced off it and reflected around the room, making the jewels on the frame sparkle so much that Jamie had to squint.

The Gnome gave a snarl and one of his feet kicked through the painting. A hand punched through another part of the canvas. His plan was working. They were about to come face to face with their enemy. . .

# CHAPTER SEVEN

# The Gnome Emerges

The Gnome thrashed about behind the painting, tearing at the holes he'd made. The bats shrieked and flapped their wings. They swirled around the room, forming a dense black cloud. The beam of torchlight shining at the mirror lit up their reflection: hundreds of beady eyes stared out.

"What are they doing?" said Milly. "They're getting ready for something."

Suddenly the bats wheeled right around, like a shoal of fish, and dived straight at the mirror, their tiny mouths open in shrieks of fury.

"They're attacking their own reflection!" Jamie realized.

A heartbeat later, the first of the bats slammed into the mirror and dropped to the floor, stunned. The rest soon followed. Their dark bodies littered the floor, some of them twitching, some moving their wings groggily. As the bats struck the glass, the jewels were dislodged and fell from the frame. They glittered among the bats' bodies.

"The stupid things have knocked themselves out," Milly said.

Without the bats' screeching it was suddenly quiet. Jamie could hear the wind shaking the trees outside, driving more rain against the windows and through the broken pane. The Gnome was quiet, too. He'd stopped punching and tearing at the canvas. Jamie saw his eyes peer out from a hole in the painting, then vanish.

Harry pulled something out of his backpack and raced over to the bat portrait. It looked like the butter knife they'd been using that afternoon. He began hacking furiously at the canvas.

"Harry!" Jamie cried. "What are you doing?"

"Come and help," Harry said. "Get him out quick, he hasn't got the bats to help him."

"Harry's right," said Milly. "We've got a better chance of defeating the Gnome without his creatures."

Jamie dropped the torch and ran with Milly to Harry. He knew his brother was brave, but this was the bravest thing he'd ever seen him do. He felt a rush of pride. He and Milly both began pulling at the ripped canvas with their hands, while Harry carried on hacking with his knife. The Gnome would have no choice but to come out.

"Handing yourselves over, are you?" came the Gnome's voice from the other side of the painting.

The canvas fell to the ground. Inside the picture frame was the Gnome. He stood in a musty, dark passageway hung with cobwebs that was set into the wall of the gallery. Jamie, Harry and Milly backed away as his bony, filthy hand gripped the side of the frame. They'd wanted to defeat him, but now – seeing him in the flesh again – Jamie couldn't help shrinking back. The Gnome's head and shoulders poked through into the gallery. His face was pinched into a scowl. Jamie could smell his horrible stench, like something rotting. The Gnome looked at the three of them, his eyes narrowed. He spat on the floor.

"Oh dear. You're all scratched. I do hope my bats haven't hurt you," he sneered.

A single bat flapped out from the passageway behind the Gnome, wheeling in circles above his head. The Gnome held out his hand and it obediently landed on his finger, hanging upside down with its wings outstretched.

"So," the Gnome snarled. "You think you've defeated my bats – but don't think you've defeated me!" He lunged forward, grabbed Harry's hair with his gnarled fingers and twisted hard, his long yellow nails scratching Harry's ears. Harry yelped.

"Leave him alone!" Jamie cried.

"Get off him!" shouted Milly.

They both pulled at the Gnome's arm. Jamie fought back his disgust at the filthy, greasy sleeve and the rotting smell. The Gnome twisted harder. Harry fell to his knees, his face screwed up in pain.

"Ha!" spat the Gnome. "Does it hurt?"

Jamie felt a wave of pure hatred wash

over him. He looked around desperately for something he could use – and noticed the glint of something shiny on the floor.

The Gnome's bat fluttered towards Milly. She managed a swift punch that left it stunned. It dragged itself across the floor to join the other bats. Jamie caught her eye and nodded towards the jewels on the floor. The torch was lying at her feet.

"I'd let you go," the Gnome said to Harry, "but I'm enjoying myself too much." He gave another twist. Harry yelped.

Jamie released his hold on the Gnome and ran across the room. He jumped to avoid the stunned bodies of the bats, and grabbed a few of the jewels. Then he held them up. Milly picked up the torch and shone it at them. They glimmered red, yellow and green.

"Look!" Jamie cried. "Jewels!"

The Gnome turned to look at Jamie. The slits of his eyes widened; his jaw fell open. He relaxed his grasp on Harry's hair. Harry ducked and scrambled away, rubbing his head.

"My treasure," croaked the Gnome. He advanced on Jamie. "Give it back to me."

# CHAPTER EIGHT

# Treasure and a Threat

Jamie turned the jewels in the light as the Gnome came towards him. The Gnome's eyes were fixed on the glittering stones, his mouth hanging open, drooling slightly. Jamie watched him carefully, while slowly backing towards the shattered sash window.

"Beautiful, aren't they?" Jamie said, making the stones catch the light.

He felt a sickening brushing sensation against his ankles. It was the bats – they were coming round from their daze and starting to move. He felt nips on his bare feet. Some of the bats pulled themselves up on to their hooked claws, giving small shrieks. Others fluttered around the ceiling. All of the creatures had their eyes fixed on the Gnome as he inched closer to Jamie, his eyes glowing dully, his bony hands reaching out for the jewels.

"Lovely, shiny treasures," he chanted, eyes wide. He looked as though he was in a daze.

Jamie waited for the Gnome to come closer . . . closer. He backed away slowly, still holding out the jewels. "Aren't they pretty," Jamie sing-songed.

The Gnome nodded, dumbly. Then he gave a sudden lunge and swiped a hand at the treasures, snarling viciously as Jamie pulled them just out of reach.

"You want them?" Jamie asked, holding the jewels above his head. "Go and get them!" He flung the jewels as hard as he could through the broken window, out into the wind and rain.

"Aargh!" shrieked the Gnome, his head snapping towards the window. "My treasure!" To Jamie's amazement, the Gnome hurled himself out of the window after the jewels, his shirt catching on the shattered glass. There was a cry of satisfaction that twisted into a shout of pain, then . . . nothing.

"He'll never have survived!" shouted Milly.

"You've done it!" Harry cried. "That's the end of him!"

The three of them ran to the window seat. Jamie felt his heart pound as he stared at the window, open-mouthed. They had seen the last of the Gnome!

Behind them, the bats in the gallery united in a terrifying screech. They streamed out of the window, the rush of their wings whistling past Jamie's ears.

"They're following the Gnome," gasped Milly.

Jamie, Harry and Milly ran to the window as the last of the bats disappeared through it. The dark cloud of terrible creatures swelled up to fill the night sky, their wings catching the moonlight.

"They're joining up!" cried Harry. "Just like the snakes!"

Harry was right. The bats were fusing together. Lots of tiny bodies became one enormous wing, and a clump of them formed a huge, ugly snout. In an instant, the creatures became one gigantic bat, dark-veined wings outstretched, swooping through the air. It let out a high-pitched scream as it sped down, moving so fast it became a blurred streak.

"It's the bat we saw in the storm," Jamie realized.

The giant bat swooped down to scoop the Gnome's body off the flagstones down below. Jamie knelt on the window seat, staring out at the bat, its dark shape silhouetted against the moon.

"Next time, you'll *really* suffer," shouted the Gnome, his evil voice reaching them through the rain. He had survived, then.

The giant bat flew off into the night. It was over.

"I thought we'd finally defeated him," Milly said. "It was so close."

"*He* nearly defeated *us*," Jamie said. Milly's face was covered in scratches. Harry's hair was sticking up in tufts, bits of it missing where the Gnome had twisted it away from his head. "Look at us. It could have been a lot worse."

"That's true," said Milly. "I thought the bats were going to drop me out of the sky."

"And I thought the Gnome was going to pull all my hair out," Harry said, touching his head. "It really hurt – and he stinks. It was horrible being that close to him."

"Even worse things might be waiting," Jamie said, sinking back against the window seat. He didn't know whether to be glad that they'd survived or frightened that the Gnome was still alive. "We haven't seen the last of him. There're still more pages in *The Book of Gnome*."

"Next time I won't let him catch me off guard," Milly said.

"Next time he'll be even angrier," Harry whispered, staring at the floor. Then he looked at Jamie and Milly. "Let's go and read *The Book of Gnome* – find out what's in store for us."

Jamie, Harry and Milly crept quietly down four flights of stairs, then through the secret passage with its carvings and cobwebs, to Granddad's study in the middle of the house.

"Look," said Jamie.

He pointed at an oval panel on the wall with five carved animals on it. The first time they'd seen it, all five animals had been in profile. After they'd met the Gnome's snake, the snake carving had turned inwards to face the room, and the same thing had happened with the Gnome's next creature, the spider. As Jamie had expected, the bat carving was now facing into the room too, its jewelled eyes glittering.

Jamie went to the great oak desk in the centre of the study and took down *The Book of Gnome*. He turned the yellowed pages to the picture of the bat. Then he took a deep breath and turned the page again.

He shuddered, and had to grip the desk to steady himself.

"Rats," said Milly. "Jamie, are you OK?"

Lightning flashed through the coloured glass in the study roof and bathed the picture of the rat in red, green and yellow light. It had huge yellow teeth and its front paws were raised as if it were about to pounce. Its long, scaly tail snaked down the page. Worst of all were its red eyes, staring out at him.

"Come on," said Harry. "Mum and Dad will wake up soon. Let's go to bed."

Jamie closed the book and followed his brother and Milly out of the room. They'd have to sneak Milly back to her cottage before everyone woke up. But when would the Gnome strike again? And could he let the others know his big secret? *There's only one thing that scares me more than the Gnome*, he thought, shuddering. *And that's rats. . .*

Now read. . .